This Little Tiger book
belongs to:

Gianna

from her Auntie Ritsa

who loves her very much

LITTLE TIGER PRESS
An imprint of Magi Publications
1 The Coda Centre, 189 Munster Road, London SW6 6AW
www.littletigerpress.com

First published in Great Britain 2008
This edition published 2008
Text copyright for: "When the Sun Goes Down to Bed"; "My Little Baby";
"Hush-a-bye, Baby"; "Bonnie Girls and Bonnie Boys"; "Stars on High";
"Hush Now, Sleepyhead" © Magi Publications 2008
Illustrations copyright © Gail Yerrill 2008
Gail Yerrill has asserted her right to be identified as the illustrator of
this work under the Copyright, Designs and Patents Act, 1988

A CIP catalogue record for this book is available from the British Library

All rights reserved • ISBN 978-1-84506-647-5
Printed in China
2 4 6 8 10 9 7 5 3 1

Illustrated by Gail Yerrill

Twinkle Twinkle Little Star

A Bedtime Book of Lullabies

LITTLE TIGER PRESS

London

Rock-a-bye Baby

Rock-a-bye baby
on the tree top.
When the wind blows
the cradle will rock.
When the bough breaks
the cradle will fall,
And down will come baby,
cradle and all.

The Owl and the Pussycat

The Owl and the Pussycat went to sea
In a beautiful pea-green boat.
They took some honey
and plenty of money,
Wrapped up in a five-pound note.

The Owl looked up to the stars above,
And sang to a small guitar,
"O, lovely Pussy! O, Pussy, my love,
What a beautiful Pussy you are,
you are, you are,
What a beautiful Pussy you are!"

Hush, Little Baby

Hush, little baby, don't say a word:
Papa's gonna buy you a mockingbird.

And if that mockingbird don't sing,
Papa's gonna buy you a diamond ring.

And if that diamond ring is brass,
Papa's gonna buy you a looking glass.

And if that looking glass gets broke,
Papa's gonna buy you a billy goat.

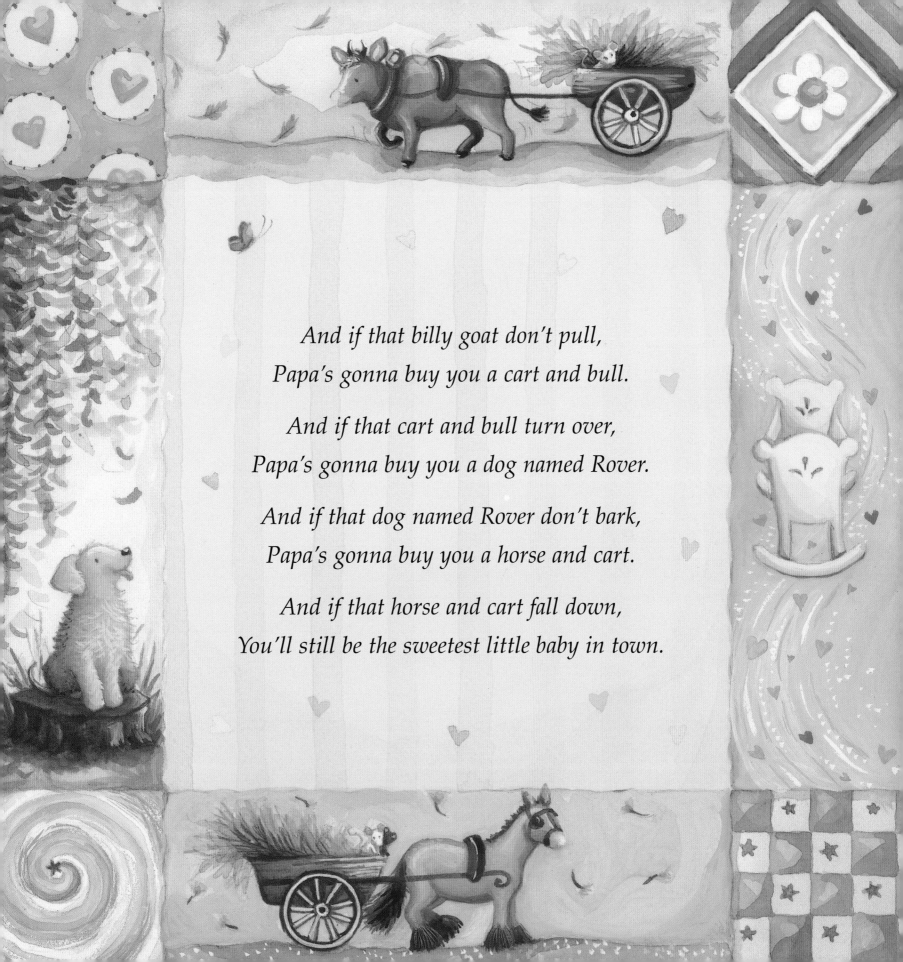

And if that billy goat don't pull,

Papa's gonna buy you a cart and bull.

And if that cart and bull turn over,

Papa's gonna buy you a dog named Rover.

And if that dog named Rover don't bark,

Papa's gonna buy you a horse and cart.

And if that horse and cart fall down,

You'll still be the sweetest little baby in town.

I See the Moon

I see the moon; the moon sees me
Under the shade of the old oak tree.
Please let the light that shines on me
Shine on the one I love.

Over the mountains, over the sea
That's where my heart is longing to be.
Please let the light that shines on me
Shine on the one I love.

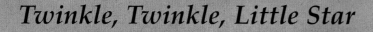

Twinkle, Twinkle, Little Star

Twinkle, twinkle, little star,
How I wonder what you are.
Up above the world so high,
Like a diamond in the sky.
Twinkle, twinkle, little star,
How I wonder what you are.

Star Light, Star Bright

Star light, star bright,
First star I see tonight.
I wish I may, I wish I might,
Have the wish I wish tonight.

When the Sun Goes Down to Bed

When the sun goes down to bed,

The stars come out to play.

They dance across the sky all night,

Until the break of day.

Lavender's Blue

Lavender's blue, dilly dilly,
Lavender's green;
When I am king, dilly dilly,
You shall be queen.

Who told you so, dilly dilly,
Who told you so?
'Twas my own heart, dilly dilly,
That told me so.

Sleep, Baby, Sleep

Sleep, baby, sleep.
Your father guards the sheep;
Your mother shakes the dreamland tree,
Down falls a little dream for thee;
Sleep, baby, sleep.

Come, Let's to Bed

"Come, let's to bed," says Sleepyhead.
"Tarry a while," says Slow.
"Put on the pan," says Greedy Nan,
"Let's sup before we go."

My Little Baby

While you sleep,
The world spins around,
Slowly to rock you,
Safe and sound.
The morning will come;
A new day will break.
And my little baby
From dreams will awake.

Come to the Window

Come to the window,
My baby with me,
And look at the stars
That shine on the sea.

There are two little stars
That play bo-peep.
And two little fish
Far down in the deep;
And two little frogs
Cry, "Neap, neap, neap."
I see a dear baby
That should be asleep!

Wee Willie Winkie

Wee Willie Winkie runs
through the town,
Upstairs and downstairs,
in his nightgown,
Tapping at the window
and crying through the lock,
"Are all the children in their beds?
It's past eight o'clock!"

Hush-a-bye, Baby

Hush-a-bye, baby,
Sleep, angel, sleep;
Warm and dry your cradle keep.
When you wake, my little one,
A new day will have just begun.

Bonnie Girls
and Bonnie Boys

Bonnie girls and bonnie boys,
Picking up their bonnie toys.
No more play, it's time for bed:
Time to rest their bonnie heads!

Stars on High

One, two – stars on high,
Three, four – in the sky,
Five, six – burning bright,
Seven, eight – in the night,
Nine, ten – I declare,
Too many stars to count up there!

Hush Now, Sleepyhead

Hush now, sleepyhead,
Lay down in your bed.
Sweet dreams all night through,
Big kiss, I love you!

All the Pretty Horses

Hush-a-bye, don't you cry,
Go to sleep, my little baby.

When you wake you will have
All the pretty little horses,
Blacks and greys, dapples and bays,
Coach and six little horses.

Hush-a-bye, don't you cry,
Go to sleep, my little baby.

Man in the Moon

The man in the moon
Looked out of the moon
And this is what he said,
"'Tis time that, now I'm getting up,
All babies went to bed!"

Brahms' Lullaby

Lullaby and goodnight,

With roses bedight,

With lilies o'er spread,

Is baby's wee bed.

Lay thee down now and rest,

May thy slumber be blessed.

Lay thee down now and rest,

May thy slumber be blessed.

All Through the Night

Sleep, my child, and peace attend thee,
All through the night.
Guardian angels God will send thee,
All through the night.

Soft the drowsy hours are creeping,
Hill and vale in slumber steeping,
I my loving vigil keeping,
All through the night.

Golden Slumbers

Golden slumbers kiss your eyes,
Smiles awake you when you rise.
Sleep, pretty darling, do not cry,
And I will sing a lullaby,
Lulla, lulla, lullaby.

Day is Done

Day is done,
Gone the sun,
From the lake, from the hills,
from the sky.
All is well, safely rest,
God is nigh.

Add some sparkle with
these twinkling Little Tiger Press titles

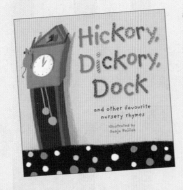

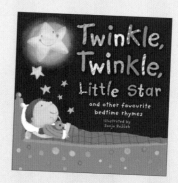

For information regarding any of the above titles
or for our catalogue, please contact us:
Little Tiger Press, 1 The Coda Centre,
189 Munster Road, London SW6 6AW
Tel: 020 7385 6333 Fax: 020 7385 7333
E-mail: info@littletiger.co.uk www.littletigerpress.com